Re-Told Traditional Tales as 'Pocket Pantomimes'

By

Don Kelly

Contents

Dedication

I would like to take a moment to express my gratitude to the many individuals who have helped me in the creation of this book. I would like to thank the team who assisted me throughout the process.

Acknowledgments

First and foremost, I would like to express my sincere gratitude to John McGrath for all his assistance and insightful feedback throughout the writing process. His helpful hints and sensible suggestions have greatly enhanced the quality of this book.

About the Author

Don Kelly dedicated many years to amateur theatre, beginning as a teenager by acting and singing in Gang Shows with the Scouts. He continued his passion for performing by portraying numerous comedic characters in various plays in various theatre groups. Don still enjoys performing now by playing the guitar, plus singing well known songs and performing his monologues either at solo gigs, or with a group of 'Strummers' at fundraising functions.. His sense of being lies in comedy, and he takes pleasure in often re-telling 'Dad Jokes' to anyone in the vicinity, resulting in their mixed reactions and groans with a smile…

Don has a married son and a married daughter, who each recently welcomed their own children, one a baby son and one a baby girl, all of whom he sees as regularly as is reasonable to suit their circumstances.

Re-Told Traditional Tales

Written as Monologues, or Raps, you to choose - it just depends on the rhythm you use

Suitable for all ages and although originally written in local areas in Lancashire, they can be in *'your town'* to be equally based anywhere at all.

They are written to be either performed solo (with the different character voices) in suitable venues, or as plays / party pieces' for all ages of Mums, Dads, sisters, brothers, nephews, nieces, Grandparents, Aunts and Uncles

For Family Fun – take turns at changing to be another of the 'Colour Coded Characters' – to see who is best at each one…

OR

Simply read to relax – and sleep with a smile

Hope you enjoy them

Jack and the Beanstalk

A Pocket-Pantomime set in *'your town'*

Optionally – the verses in Italics could be omitted when being 'performed' if considered making the performance 'too long'

Character/speech voices – Narrator, Mother, Jack, Bird, Giant, Policeman

I'm going to tell you a story, about a young lad called Jack

It's a story that happened in *'your town'* a couple of months ago back

His Ma had sent him to market, to go and trade in their cow

But when he came back with no money, his Ma and Jack had a row

'Eee lad whatever has happened, what happened when you went out
You know we needed that money, and now you've come back with nowt'
'But Ma, I met with this feller, and he told me a marvellous tale
About magic beans in his pocket, and for the cow, he'd make me a sale'

'Well I thought about what he'd told me, I mean, being magic and all
Them beans made a nice proposition, so I tied up the cow to his stall'
'But lad it's money we're needing' not just a bag of old beans
So come on lad, give them to me, come on get them out of your jeans

Well, as you can see she were nowty, after listening to all that he'd said
And she threw them there beans out o' window, and sent the poor lad off to bed
Now next morning when Jack had awoken, he was feeling a little bit ill
So he thought that today he'd not bother, to get up to go down to the mill

But just then his Ma came in running, all excited said 'Jack come and see'
So he got up and went to the window and there was a ruddy big 'tree'
'Well by gum mum where's that from, it don't half go up right high
Hey, them beans were magic, I told you, and look they've grown up to the sky'

'You know lad I'm sorry what happened, when I sent you to bed last night
But when you came back with no money, it gave me a terrible fright'
But now lad we're going to be famous, there's one heck of a crowd outside
They've all come to see what's happened, with that tree growing up to the sky'

Do you mean we'll be in the *local paper*? and maybe on telly as well?

With pictures and stories about us, hey Ma you never can tell'

'Lad I think it would be an idea if you were to climb up that tree

As then we could **sell** them a story, about everything you could see

We could sell the story tomorrow, assuming you're not up there too long

So come on lad get your clothes on, there's money to make, get it done'

So his mother made him some butties, with a great big flask full of tea

And Jack went outside with his clogs on, and started climbing his tree.

The crowd outside started cheering, as he shouted 'I'll see you tonight'

Then off he went up his beanstalk, until he was clean out of sight

……………………………………………………..………………………..

Option to omit this next section in italics' if it is considered 'too long' for overall performance

……………………………………………………………………………

When he got to the top he was shattered, and was panting and red in the face

So he stood stock-still by a stone-style, to take a good look at the place

Now though he was feeling light headed, he hoped he was dreaming or drunk

As everything round him seemed massive, either that, or through climbing, he'd shrunk

There he was at the side of a castle, made of stone with a 30-foot door

So, as he couldn't reach the knocker, he nipped-in through a hole in the floor

Inside it was nice, fully furnished, with rooms off a main central isle

But cold with very high ceilings, sort of early Dracula style

Then the ground where he stood started shaking, as footsteps came in down the hall

And joined to each foot at the ankle, was a giant 20 feet tall

In his hands there was flapping and thrashing, from an angry white feathered bird

But the giant ignored it to listen, to something he thought he had heard

He sniffed the air and looked round him, and his deep voice said, 'Fee Fi Fo Fum'

Which loosely translates into English, as, 'Blood of an English man'

Now Jack, being quick on the uptake, thought he'd better keep out of his way

Or he might get stood on and flattened, which he reckoned would spoil his day

But just at that moment, which helped him, the bird without making a sound

After raising itself and straining, laid an egg which fell to the ground

Now by rights, thought Jack, from that distance, and especially still being raw

That egg should have broken on impact, but instead, it cracked the floor

It bounced once or twice on the paving, then slowly passed Jack it rolled

Where much to his amazement, he could see it was made out of gold

As the giant bent down to fetch it, the bird fell free from his grasp

And ran to where Jack was hiding, who then reckoned he'd breathed his last

'Come on, let's escape from this giant', said the bird from the side of his beak

Which surprised Jack, as you'd imagine, as he didn't know birds could speak

'Let's go then' said Jack quickly thinking, as he ran out across the floor

'Be quick now, get him distracted - fly at him while I get the door'

And so they escaped from the giant, by running for all they were worth

To get them both back to the beanstalk' sticking up through the hole in the earth

……………………………………………………………

Close the omission of the verses in italics

....

It was about then his mother got worried and wondered just when he'd come back

'As she didn't have any husband, only her lad - young Jack

She decided to get some assistance, and so for a policeman she sent

As Jack had gone up this beanstalk' and nobody knew where it went

Well this 'Copper' came and he asked her, 'Now tell me what's going on here

Just give me the story right slowly, so all the *facts* I'll get clear'

She told him all that had happened, about the beans and then how

She'd thrown them out of the window, while they were having a row…

'By gum lass' he said 'that's some story' When she had finished her tale

'Are you sure that these are *facts* lass, or have you been 'supping the ale?'

'Well look outside for yourself lad, and you'll see out there the beanstalk'

So after a slight hesitation, off to the window he walked

It was then that he saw something moving, and he wondered what it could be

'I think it maybe your Jack coming home lass, come to the window and see'

By now the figure was closer, and she saw that it was her Jack

So she ran outside and she shouted, 'Eee lad, I'm so glad you're back'

Then Jack jumped down from the beanstalk, said the Copper 'now let's have the facts'

But Jack pushed him aside as he shouted, 'quick mother (gulp) get an axe'

They wondered why all this commotion, as Jack started chopping the tree

But then as they looked up the beanstalk, all the trouble now they could see

A great big giant was coming, and he looked proper angry and mad

Said Jack 'It's me that he's after' said mother 'Eee what's happened lad'

Now the giant was coming down quickly, but not too quick for our Jack

Having chopped through the tree it was falling, and the giant fell dead on his back

'By gum that was close' said his mother, 'We needed that bit of good luck

But tell me lad why was he chasing' said Jack 'I've stolen his duck'

They went in the house for some cocoa, the story for Jack to unfold

About this duck that he'd stolen, a duck that lays eggs of gold

And then young Jack and his mother, to the papers the story they sold

But without giving mention to anyone, about the ducks' eggs being gold

They figured if anyone knew it, they'd get 'begging letters' and such

So they kept that one bit of the story, between them without saying much

But they told them the rest of the story, it was broadcast on telly one night

Then they wrote a book and made a film, got a fortune from the copy write

They bought a big house in the suburbs, and if ever they are hard-up

They go into town for some money, with a golden egg from their duck

So…. if it's fame and its riches you're after, and you fancy the life of your dreams

Take a cow to your local market, to the chap who sells magic beans

Cinderella

A Pocket-Pantomime set in *'your town'*

Character/speech voices – Narrator, Cinders, Mother, Woman, Albert, Father

In a rundown estate in *'your town'*, lived a family who rose up to fame

By the fortune of their youngest daughter, who was called Cinderella by name

Now Cinders worked in a factory, and like any working class lass

She hated her job, but it paid well, so she only stayed for the 'brass'

But each day while she was working, her daydreams and visions she made

As how, with luck, she would one day, get out of her spot-welders trade

At brew time and at dinner hour, she would pass the time away

By thinking of her dream lover who worked in a mill down the way

But it wasn't a 'shop-floor' worker, that her eyes were set upon

But none other than Albert Pritchard, who was the 'mill owners' son

At last her chance came one summer, when her firm held a beauty contest

So she entered, and though she was nervous, she stood as much chance as the rest

The prize was just what she wanted, tickets for the Annual Dance

And knowing that Albert would be there, to meet him would be her big chance

Now this beauty show, held in the factory, was attended by most just for fun

Just to see all the men and the women, coming out with their '***Sunday best***' clothes on

They'd a comedian for some amusement, and everyone had a good laugh

Then enjoyed the beer and the 'nibbles', laid on by the office staff

Then the judging was done without trouble, and soon got the girls down to three

There was Cinders, a shorthand-typist, and the boss's secretary

They had all the girls parading, then spoke to them one by one

And after they'd chatted the others, Cinderella's turn had come

The others had spoken so proper that Cinders wasn't sure what to say

But she just smiled then plucked up some courage, and said "it's been a great day"

They asked her where she came from, and what she liked doing most

So she said that she came from *'your town'* and liked to visit the coast

They left to make their decision, which gave time to put on the *'turns'*

For entertaining the masses, while inside our Cinders 'burned'

Eventually the judges, came back and went on the stage

To stop the comic and talking, to give the decision they'd made

They gave the third prize to a typist, and the second prize was to come

To the boss's secretary, which meant that Cinders had won

She wept with joy when she heard it, and ran to the man with the prize

To take the works-dance tickets, while happy tears ran from her eyes

The evening eventually ended, and Cinders got changed and went home

To tell her Father and Mother, that their youngest daughter had won

"Eee what did you win?" said her Mother, "was it something we can all share?"

"It's tickets to the Annual dance, but I don't think you'd fit in there"

"Of course we would" shouted Father. "Do you think we're not good enough

To rub shoulders with all them' hob-nob's, We'll show them that we're not rough"

"And just for your cheek and insolence, you can give them tickets to me

Just how many tickets were there?" and Cinders answered, "Three"

"What a funny number" said Mother. "But not as funny as this"

Said Father as he tore up the third one "Cinderella this dance you will miss"

For the second time that evening Cinderella broke down into tears

For her cruel Father and Mother had done her strongest fears

She knew it were no use trying, to make them change their mind

So she went to bed deflated, wondering why they were so unkind

The Saturday of the dance night, at last it came around

And Cinders was washing up dishes, when her Father and Mother came down

They were dressed up like a 'dog's dinner', and with top hat and tails to his coat

Father pranced in front of the mirror, then with a vicious tongue he spoke

"Now when you've washed them dishes, and you've cleaned and polished the car

You can get yourself in the kitchen, to work as the cleaner you are

To think you even considered, that you could go to the dance

And that dress you wear is so scruffy, to get in, you don't have a chance"

It was useless for Cinders to argue, as each week they took her wage

And gave her what they considered, enough for a girl of her age

But ten pound a week for working, while they were both on the dole

Seemed cruel and made saving harder, to buy dresses or any such goal

So, dejected she did all her chores, and forgot of her dream love Albert

Then sat down to watch the Telly, when her senses came alert

She thought at first she was dreaming, for appearing out of the gloom

Was a woman all dressed up in sequins, and the brightness filled up the room

"What the heck's going on" said Cinders, as she jumped up out of her chair
"One minute I'm sat watching Telly, and the next, your stood standing there!"
"I'm sorry if a gave you a shock love, I'm just on my way to the Dance
 I'm from the 'Welders' Union', so I've called in for your 'subs', by chance"

Well this was the last straw on a camel, and Cinders swiftly saw red
And in anger she flew at the woman, who then slipped and banged her head
She'd knocked the woman unconscious, but then seeing they were the same size
Cinders took the dress off the woman, and decided to claim her firm's prize

She had a quick wash and brush-up, and had the dress on in a flash
Then rooted around in the pockets, for the ticket and any spare cash
But knowing that she would be angry, if she woke up to find that she'd gone
Cinders put a cushion, under her head, to ensure that she would sleep on

She reckoned in about six hours, the woman would wake, mad as hell
So she planned to return for midnight, as it was just six o'clock when she fell
Her car was parked by the curbside, with the keys in, all ready to go
So Cinders in need of transporting, climbed in and set off to the show

It was then as she drove to the dance hall, she realised what she had done
She felt guilty, but then it was too late, and may as well finish off, now begun
On arrival she felt a bit nervous, but remembering Albert was there
She marched to the front of the Dance Hall, and determined like, climbed the stair

Keeping wide her eyes for Albert, but more so for 'Mum and Dad'

For if they saw she'd attended, the scene, would have been, pretty bad

But at last across the ballroom, two pairs of eyes met mid space

The eyes of Albert and Cinders, each wanting to meet face to face

Cinderella smiled first, then turned, playing at hard to get

But Albert, undaunted, came running, to the face he'd never forget.

They danced and danced through the evening, just looking in each other's eyes

And Cinders forgot what the time was, just having got her 'prize'

But soon the hours passed by them, 'till the band had all but stopped

Then she realised what the time was, and hoped the car wasn't blocked

It was then both Albert and Cinders, looked down for the first time that night

And when Cinders saw her footwear, she all but died of fright…

To come dancing and driving away, from the woman she'd had to nobble

She'd come out in her red woolly slippers, each complete with a furry bobble!

She turned and fled from Albert, and with tears running down her face

Didn't see that she'd lost a slipper, as she ran to her parking space

She got in the car and vanished, and Albert, looking proper upset

Bent down and picked up the slipper, that belonged to the girl he'd just met

But there inside the slipper, was a tab that gave her name

And also gave an address, number twenty-seven, Church Lane

Meanwhile our Cinders was turning, into that very same street

And at twenty-seven she pulled up, and went in the house discreet

The Union woman was sleeping, so Cinders not making a sound

Got changed and re-dressed the lady, then started bringing her round

She woke with a start, then slowly, and carefully tried to recall

How she'd got on the floor, so Cinders said, that she'd 'just had a fall'

Then after some coffee and biscuits, the lady left quite intact

Except that she'd lost her evening, not knowing it had been 'hijacked'

Cinders went to bed as her Mother, and Father, were due to come home

And she'd just gone to sleep with her memories, when they called her up to come down

 For downstairs, there was her Albert, with his motor car parked outside

And there was Cinders in rollers, who with embarrassment, almost cried

"I don't care about wealth and riches, as those I've got of my own

Marry me and we'll live together, and in a "posher part of the town"

"Oh, yes please Albert" she answered "But first can you explain

How you found out where to find me - did you see the slipper in the drain?"

So Cinders gave up 'spot welding', for her dream love she'd managed to land

And happily ever after, they lived in a mansion so grand

And Albert being kind and thoughtful, Got the mother and father employed

In writing this fairy tale story, with the fame we've all since enjoyed.

Aladdin

A Pocket-Pantomime set in *'your town'*

Character/speech voices – Narrator, Aladdin, Genie, Miss Clamp

I'll tell you a Chinese story that started one dark Friday night

ln a chip shop in *'your town'* just up by the station, on the right

Now this Chinese take-away chippy, was owned by a Mr. Addin

And because his first name was Alan, he was known as Al Addin

His hobby was buying old lanterns, especially the Chinese type

And he hung them in the shop window, to make the atmosphere right

Now this Friday night he was serving, some sweet and sour chicken with rice

When a customer happened to mention, he thought his lanterns looked nice

At that Al smiled and nodded, and gave a deep Chinese-type bow

Then answered the comment by saying "Aye, they're not bad 'happen as how"

The customer seemed quite surprised, after hearing the way that Al spoke

And asked the owner about it, so Al explained to the bloke

"I was born and bred here in *'your town'*, though me parents came from afar,

So I've an 'oriental' look about me, that I got from me Ma and Pa

But I can't use a 'foreign' accent, I tried it but soon had to stop

Cos me mates just burst out laughing' when they heard me talk in the shop"

They got chatting and the customer showed him, a lantern he'd bought that day

On the market from an local seller, for just ten Pounds he'd had to pay

"By gum that's a bargain you got there", said Al looking closer at it

"Just needs a bit of a clean-up, with elbow grease, polish and spit"

"Look, I like that lantern I tell yer, and me words I'm not one to mix

I'll give you your Ten quid if you'll sell it, and I'll throw in a free bag of chips"

The man agreed and they parted, both of them pleased with their gain.

And Al carefully examined his purchase, while holding it up by the chain.

He saw on the base some writing, then read it and felt such a fool

Al knew right away it wasn't real, as it said, *'Made in Liverpool'*

But he reckoned if he hadn't read it, the difference he'd never have guessed

So he decided to clean it anyway, and hang it up with the rest.

He closed-up the shop for the evening and a place on the table he cleared

And had just got to work with polishing, when a big *'Scouse'* Genie appeared

"What the heck's going on?" said Al Addin, an astounded look on his face

But the Genie just smiled and answered "Are you talkin' to me there Ace?"

"l've been stuck in that lantern for ages, 'oping someone would give it a rub

An' l tell yer - l'm ruddy well starvin', can you spare me a pint and some grub?"

"Well happen you're in a chip shop, so l reckon some food l can do,

But I can't help out with a pint lad, though a pot of tea I can brew"

"Yea, ta, you're a really nice feller, and for getting me out of there

l've got lucky powers inside me, and three wishes l can grant yer"

"So 'urry up with the cookin' and think about what you'd like

A house, a car, anything, a wife or a big motorbike?"

So Al prepared all the cooking, and made a big pot of tea

Then watched the lot get guzzled, by the hungry scouse Genie

"You know what l really fancy", said Al after thinking' a time

"lt's something l've always wanted, but never thought could be mine"

"Just say the word and l'll give it.. l'm not pullin' your leg our kid

I will pay anything that you ask me, from a Rolls to a million Quid"

"l'll tell you what l want then, and me dreams l hope you won't daunt

But instead of a Chinese chippy, l'd like a big restaurant

Now it's got to be grand and successful, the best for miles around

With a doorman and a great big car park, and in a posher part of town

And to help me with the accounting, l'd like for me second wish

A wife who's a good head for money, and also a bit of a 'dish'

And to go with me wife and restaurant, for the third part of the bargain you made

l want to be rich and famous, but respected throughout the trade"

"Like I said before, that's no problem, all those l can make sure you get

Just leave it to me Al Addin, I'll do it without breaking a sweat"

Then the Genie went back in the lantern, and Al went off to bed

And hoped the Genie wasn't lying, about everything that he'd said

But next day in the post came a letter, about an Uncle who'd been very ill

And it said his uncle had 'passed on', and left Al, his house, in his will

"Well blooming heck" said Al Addin "That mansion of his, it were grand

Just out of town, with a nice long drive, and a couple of acres of land"

"l can sell me shop and from the proceeds, fit this new place out

Converting it into a restaurant…that Genie didn't hang about"

Then he went to an Estate Agent, and got struck by love at the door

By the lass sat behind the counter, who he fancied like no-one before

It's all coming true, thought Al, and his luck was beginning to thank

Then she spoke and Al was in deeper, "Good Morning" she said "I'm Miss Clamp"

For a minute he stood there dumfounded, not knowing quite what to say

But Miss Clamp in a business-like manner, soon got the deal under way

When the contract they had completed, Al thought he'd follow a hunch

So he said "Miss Clamp, to celebrate, will you come to the pub for some lunch?"

"Why yes, Mr Addin I'd like to, we could go to the 'Buckle and Badge'

And to make it a little more friendly, I'd like you to call me Madge"

"And call me Al" he answered, then off they went to the pub

Where they got to know each better, over drinks, and good tasty grub

Al told her about his business and what for the future he planned

And because he would need some assistance, he asked if she'd give him a hand

Her reply was a forgone conclusion, for of course, she said that she would

So to sort it and make the arrangements, they met as much as they could

Now with having these regular meetings, it became just a matter of time

Until they fell for each other and Al asked 'Madgi… will you be mine?'

She agreed and so they got married, and became a husband and spouse

And got busy with their restaurant, converted from his uncle's house

They gained a good reputation and customers came by the score

And from parking they were admitted, by a man holding open the door

And so the three lucky wishes, of the Genie had come true

For Al got his Chinese restaurant, and his good-looking business wife too

And of course, as you know, they got famous, and that Genie we'd all like to thank,

For their fame is through this very story of… Al Addin and his Madgi Clamp…

Red Riding Hood

A Pocket-Pantomime set in *'your town'*

Character speech voices – Narrator, Wolf, Red Riding Hood, Granny

In the outskirts area of *'your town'* lived a girl known as 'Red Riding Hood'

Who each weekend went to her Granny's, who lived further out in a wood

And it was on one sunny morning, that this tale first began

As she set off to go to the bus stop, on the way to visit her Gran

She was walking down the high street, just minding her business like
When a wolf drew up beside her, sat astride a big motorbike.
"Where are you going to Angel", he asked with a lecherous leer
"I'll give you a lift on my pillion, jump on and I'll take you there"

"No thanks" Red Riding Hood answered, "I'd rather get on the bus"
Then set off again down the high street, to walk to the terminus
The wolf watched her for a few minutes, as she walked on down the street
Then gave a long wolf whistle, to show her he thought she looked sweet

Red smiled but carried on walking, then the wolf rode up once again
To try and get her talking, and started by asking her name
She knew she was backing a loser, and to ignore him wouldn't be good
So she said "With a hyphenated surname - I'm called Red Riding-Hood"

I know I was cheeky for asking, but thanks for telling me Red
And just in case you were wondering, my friends all call me Fred"
"To get to know you better, I'll give you that lift, if you like
And take you wherever you're going, on the back of my big motorbike"

"Well thanks, but no" Red answered, "I really don't think that I will,
As I'm going to visit my Granny, who is laid up in bed as she's ill"
"And to turn up there on her doorstep, with a bloke I only just met,
I don't think that she would like it, and may start to worry and fret"

"So, I'll go there on my own thanks, if it's all he same to you

And I must get down to the bus stop, as I reckon the bus is now due"

The wolf sat there awhile and waited, 'til the bus had been and gone

And was wondering when he'd next see her, when an idea he hit upon

 For a wolf the scheme was cunning, and as crafty as a wily old fox,

And he smiled to himself as he got off his bike, to find a telephone box

He very soon came upon one, and didn't have far to look

For the addresses of the 'Riding-Hoods', in the local telephone book

Having got the info, he needed, he went back to his motorized 'steed'

And set off to go to her Granny's, riding at a high speed

On arrival we went through the doorway, and pretending that he was 'Red'

He shouted upstairs to her Granny, "I'm here Gran, are you still in bed?"

"Yes love, I am" she answered, "take off your coat and come up

There's still a drink left in the teapot, so bring yourself up a cup"

The wolf then took off his leathers, his gloves and crash helmet too,

Then went upstairs to her bedroom, and as a nasty joke shouted 'Boo'

Now he hadn't meant to harm her but being so old and so frail

She fainted of fright at seeing him, turning cold and stiff and pale

Not thinking that this could have happened, he was sorry for what he had done

And stood there not knowing what's better, whether to stay or to run

But with Red Riding-Hood coming, not expecting her to be dead,

He thought that he'd better fool her, so hid Granny under the bed

He then took her shawl and nightcap, and put powder over his face

And covered himself with the bed-clothes, ready to take her place

In no time at all Red got there, and shouted "Hello Gran I'm here"

And the wolf, in his best Granny accent, said "Hello, come on upstairs my dear"

She went upstairs to the bedroom, and into the doorway she stood

Then seeing the change in her Granny, said "Eee, you're not looking so good! "

"Your eyes have gone right massive, big ears and a tail and all,

You're not looking right, I tell you, I think your Doctor I'll call"

At hearing a Doctor was coming, the wolf got a bit of a fright

"But I feel a lot better like this love, I can hear and see you alright"

"And don't worry about my mouth love, It's just a bit swollen and sore

So forget about the Doctor, an aspirin will do for a cure"

Red picked up the phone to ignore 'her', and had just got the dialing tone

When she realised it wasn't her Granny, so she clobbered him with the phone

Rubbing his head it was obvious, that he was caught out so he ran

But Red didn't try to chase him, but looked round the room for her Gran

She found her under the bedstead, all covered with dust and muck

So she pulled her on to the carpet, and started cleaning her up

She got her comfy and breathing, and gently brought her round

Till she opened her eyes and said "Hello love…. why am I on the ground?"

"You've had a bit of a shock Gran, but don't worry, you're OK

Lie still while I get your Doctor, he'll soon be on his way"

Then the wolf got caught and quickly, was put in the local jail,

Where he spent his time just cursing, that he hadn't hidden his tail

So take care all you young ladies, when you give a man your name

As it might be at your Granny's, that you meet up again…

Goldilocks and the Three Bears

A Pocket-Pantomime set in '*your town*'

Character/speech voices – Narrator, Goldilocks, Father'Ton', Mother'Tu', Son'Teddy'

Very early on one Sunday morning, from a party gone on through the night

Goldilocks was staggering homewards, not feeling, altogether, quite right

While feeling a little unsteady, with a head that was starting to pound

She wanted to walk no further, but sleep, right there, on the ground

Her home was a long, long journey, on the other side of a wood

And she just wanted to get there quickly, and in bed as soon as she could

She thought she'd try out a short cut, to see if she would get there quicker

But alas, with no path to follow, she got lost as the thicket got thicker

She tried going back but 'twas useless, and went around in circles, poor girl

And having lost her sense of direction, her head was just all in a whirl

But then through the trees was a clearing, where a strange looking cottage stood

Made of tin cans and boxes and bottles, held together with odd bits of wood

Goldilocks walked up to it thinking, "*It's like something that's come from afar*

And I think I can look inside it" for she saw that the door was a *'jar'*

The cottage appeared to be empty, so she shouted "Is anyone home?"

But silence came back as the answer, so she ventured inside all alone

The settee in the lounge was empty, and she thought "*Well 'sofa' so good*"

Then she saw in the kitchen a table, where three bowls of porridge were stood.

Now the sight of this food made her hungry, but she wasn't quite sure what to do

For names were inscribed on the bowls, there was 'Teddy' and 'Ton' and 'Tu'

The sizes were small, large and medium, all hot – as steam rose off all three

They were clearly somebody's breakfast, but who and where could they be?

Her stomach started to rumble, and though she knew it was wrong

She decided to sample the big one, but too hot and it burnt her tongue

She looked round the kitchen for water, where a pail she found by the door
Which soon cooled down her burning mouth, not having such *'hot lips'* before
Feeling better but still feeling hungry, she tried the medium sized bowl
And more carefully sampled the contents, but found that, alas, was too cold

The small one was next to be tasted, which proved not too cold or too hot
So, with a well-practiced right arm motion, she managed to finish the lot
Her head was still sore and aching, though better for being fed
But still she felt exhausted, so she set off in search of a bed

Upstairs she found a selection, of three, on which she could rest
One large, one small and one medium, but the smallest one suited her best
For a while she lay there thinking, of all that she'd just been through
For somehow it all seemed familiar, but just thought it was Deja vu

Meanwhile in the heart of the forest, chopping firewood using an axe
Were the three bears from the cottage, so I give you now the *bear* facts
The mother's name was 'Tu' and the father's name was 'Ton'
And helping with the firewood was, a small one 'Teddy', their son

'While Teddy and Ton had been chopping, Tu was further afield,
Finding food and little 'presents', which she kept in a basket concealed
"Now it's time to go" said 'Ton' "come on let's get to the lair
To have our breakfast porridge, and the 'gifts' that you've brought 'Tu bear"

So off they went to the cottage, for the breakfast's, they'd left to cool

As it was getting near time that Teddy, had to set off to go to school.

They got back and took off their jackets, and hung them behind the front door

And Tu in her motherly manner, wished they could afford some more

For father's old jacket was tattered, and stuffing hung out here and there

"We'll have to get new ones soon dear, just look at this *Padding Ton bear*"

They decided to go for their breakfast, and went through to the kitchen

Where it wasn't for wanting their coats, they felt cold on their *bear skin*

"Who's been eating my porridge?" said Ton, "And mine" said mother *Tu*

"And mine's <u>all</u> gone" said Teddy, "but you've got *some* - it's all right for you"

"Don't worry" said father, "we'll find them, let's have a good look round our lairs"

So they looked round the lounge and kitchen, and after that went upstairs

"Someone's been in my bed" said Mother, "and mine too" said Dad getting mad

Then Teddy on seeing his own bed' said, "You're not going to believe this Dad!"

And on seeing Goldilocks sleeping, Father said "this had better be good"

"I don't know where she's from" said Teddy "I was out with you getting wood"

"Yes he was" said Mother quickly, "he's been with us all the time"

"She must be the porridge-pincher, so get those '*doubts*' of yours off your mind"

"OK then" said Father", let's wake her, to see what she's doing here"

"Yes and get my porridge back off her, my school time is getting near"

Now with all this talk in the bedroom, Goldilocks woke with a fright

And on seeing three bears stood round her, knew something wasn't quite right

'What sort of hangover is this - that drink must have been very strong

I've heard of seeing pink elephants, but not Teddy Bears, something is wrong'

Then seeing that she had awoken, Ton bear said "Who are you, explain"

'Now one's talking to me', thought Goldilocks, and vowed never to drink again

But explain she did to the trio, telling them how she'd got lost

And said 'sorry' for eating the porridge, and offered to pay for the cost

But the bears on hearing her story, took pity on her then and there

And gave her a great big bear hug, with a cuddle off Teddy Bear

"We'll take you to the edge of the forest, while we take young Teddy to school

But he'll have to go without breakfast, there's no time for a new one to cool"

"But Mum I want some porridge, I can't learn on an empty tum

Aw, let me have some porridge, go on please, please make me some"

"I can't Teddy I'm sorry, now come on, it's getting late

Wash your hands and feet and hurry, attend to your paws while we wait"

Then Teddy complaining of hunger, and Goldilocks, whose head was still sore

Went back to their lives, as normal, after waving goodbye at the door.

Milton Keynes UK
Ingram Content Group UK Ltd.
UKHW051923310823
427861UK00006B/47